LAU

JAKE AND THE THIEF OF CLUCKINGHAM PALACE

With Phil Callaway
Drawings by Sharon Dahl
Colour by Laugh Again

This book is a product of Laugh Again, a ministry of The Good News Broadcasting Association of Canada. For more products from Laugh Again and Phil Callaway in Canada or worldwide, please visit laughagain.ca, call 1-800-663-2425, or email info@laughagain.ca. For more products from Laugh Again and Phil Callaway in the United States, please visit laughagain.us, call 1-844-663-2424, or email info@gngm.org.

Content © 2024 Phil Callaway. Publication © 2024 The Good News Broadcasting Association of Canada. Published by The Good News Broadcasting Association of Canada.

No part of this publication may be reproduced, distributed, or transmitted in any form or by any means, including photocopying, recording, or other electronic or mechanical methods, without the prior written permission of the publisher, except in the case of brief quotations embodied in critical reviews and certain other noncommercial uses permitted by copyright law. For permission requests, permissions@gnbac.ca

THE HOLY BIBLE, NEW INTERNATIONAL VERSION®, NIV® Copyright © 1973, 1978, 1984, 2011 by Biblica, Inc.™ Used by permission. All rights reserved worldwide.

ISBN (Paperback) 978-1-998048-13-7
ISBN (Hardcover) 978-1-998048-22-9
ISBN (E-book) 978-1-998048-21-2

DEDICATION:

For Seth and Caleb, Noah and Liam.
Proof that brothers can be friends too.

REMEMBER:

Fear is like a big baby.
It grows when you nurse it.

CONTENTS

1 Scrambled Eggs and a Slithering Escape

4 The Cluckingham Palace Mystery

9 The Slithery Bandit

12 Late-Night Fears and Bedtime Prayers

16 Jake's Eggscellent Plan

20 The Thief's Sneaky Surprise

24 My Prayer

25 My Very First Song

26 Jake's Goodnight Prayer

27 Jake's Wake-Up Prayer

SCRAMBLED EGGS AND A SLITHERING ESCAPE

There are three things I don't like at all. Scrambled eggs. Climbing trees. And snakes. My big brother Jake loves all three. He loves eggs every morning. Poached eggs. Soft-boiled eggs. Hard-boiled eggs. And eggs once-over-with-a-bump. He likes climbing oak trees any old time of the year. He likes holding snakes, talking to them, and giving them names. We were doing dishes together one night and talking about these things.

"Hey," he said, sliding a dirty plate into the soapy sink, "you didn't finish your eggs."

"They're yuk," I said. "They taste like slugs from the garden."

"They're good for what ails you," said Jake.

"Slugs are good for you?"

"No!" he laughed. "Eggs. Eggs are *egg-citing!*" Then he couldn't stop laughing. Often Jake finds himself quite funny. "Tomorrow I'll show you the best way to eat them." Then he frowned and whispered, "Did you hear that a snake climbed out of Mrs. Wilson's toilet yesterday and she's moving out of town?"

"The snake is moving out of town?"

I don't know why he laughed. "Mrs. Wilson," he said. "Not the snake."

"You mean the Mrs. Wilson down the road?" I was scrubbing disgusting yellow stuff from my plate.

"Yup," said my big brother. "The snake's loose near our farm now. Little kids should stay indoors."

"I'm not a little kid," I said, still stabbing at the egg. "What kind of snake is it?"

"A black mamba," said Jake. "It's from the zoo, I guess. They don't usually live around here."

"What's a black mamba?"

"It's big, it's mean, and it's fast," said my brother. "We learned about them in school. The world record is 14 feet. They can hang from ceilings or drop from trees. And they especially love chicken eggs. They show up just about anywhere. In toilets and drainpipes and sometimes in the sink."

I pulled my hands from the water very fast and squinted at the soapy suds. "Chicken eggs, huh? What are we gonna do about it?" I moved away from the sink, but kept an eye on it.

"We're gonna watch the chicken coop, that's what we're gonna do."

"I'll pay you five bucks to put your hands in the sink and finish my dishes," I said.

Jake laughed.

I stopped scrubbing the counter and stared out the window. "Mom told me to have a bath tonight," I said. "You don't think a snake could get in our bathtub, do you?"

"Na," said Jake. "They would rather take a shower."

TO THINK ABOUT:

Name three foods that aren't your favourite.

Name three foods that are your favourite.

Would you put your hands into the sink for five dollars?

What is one thing you like about Jake?

TO SMILE ABOUT:

Q: Why do French people like to eat snails?
A: Because they don't like fast food!

TO MEMORIZE:

"For the Spirit God gave us does not make us timid, but gives us power, love and self-discipline."

2 Timothy 1:7 (NIV)

THE CLUCKINGHAM PALACE MYSTERY

That night the sky was a canvas painted with bright globs of red and orange. The sun was burning holes in it as we climbed the old oak tree behind our house. I was scared to death I'd fall. "Don't look down," said my brother, as he scrambled up behind me. "Hang on tight. You'll be fine."

If I tilted my head to one side and peeked through the tree branches, I could see the chicken coop. Jake and I were proud of that coop. We had spent all of June building it. Crafting little doorways and windows. Building little ladders for the chickens to climb, so they could try to fly. A wire fence kept it safe from thieving weasels and rascally raccoons. We painted it red and white, hooked up real electricity and hung a hand-painted sign: "Cluckingham Palace."

Jake was talking about how eggs had gone missing, but I wasn't listening.

"We should put a TV in it," I suggested, "not just a light. It would give the chickens something to do." But Jake said no, they needed their sleep. "Chickens that watch too much TV forget to lay eggs. You just wait, little brother. We'll sell their eggs at the market and make our first million."

I wondered what we would do with a million dollars. Maybe buy more chickens. Dad worked hard, but there wasn't much money.

"Do you know what happened when the chicken ate gunpowder?" Jake asked. I didn't know.

"He *eggs-ploded*."

It didn't take me long to get the joke and when I did, I had to hang tightly to the branch so I didn't fall.

"Know why chickens get up so early?" he asked.

"Nope."

"Because they always set their alarm *clucks*."

We sat in silence as I thought about that one.

"I like the dark," said Jake.

"Why's that?"

"It's the only time I can see the stars. And did you know that the sun is brighter than 14 trillion fireflies?"

I didn't know that. And I didn't know where Jake came up with these things. He is the smartest kid I've ever met.

"I was reading about snakes at school," he continued, "and I learned some pretty cool stuff."

"Like what?" I asked, staring straight ahead. The sun was brushing its teeth and saying goodnight as it slowly melted into the purple hills.

"Well, for one thing, there aren't any snakes in Ireland, New Zealand, or Newfoundland. And rattlesnakes can't hear the sound of their own rattles."

"Black mambas don't have rattles, do they?"

"Nope," said Jake, "just big fangs."

I was looking down for the first time. "Do you think black mambas can climb trees?"

Jake said they could. That they sometimes looked for food in oak trees. "You're not scared, are you?" he asked.

"Well…" I shrugged, "maybe a little."

"Don't worry," he grinned. "They bite you and you'll see stars, but you won't feel much after that."

I hung even tighter onto the branches and stared at the horizon.

All was quiet in Cluckingham Palace. Then I heard a noise. "Maybe their alarm clucks woke them up," said Jake.

TO THINK ABOUT:

Which chicken joke did you like best?

Should they put a TV in the chicken coop?
Why? Or why not?

Who should we tell when things frighten us?

TO SMILE ABOUT:

Jake: Knock, knock.
Me: Who's there?
Jake: Chicken.
Me: Chicken Who?
Jake: Just chicken to see who's in there.

TO MEMORIZE:

"The Lord is my light and my salvation—whom shall I fear? The Lord is the stronghold of my life—of whom shall I be afraid?"

Psalm 27:1

THE SLITHERY BANDIT

My big brother stopped grinning, put a finger to his lips and shushed me. The chickens grew restless. The clucking grew louder. "It's the kind of noise a chicken makes when its eggs are being stolen," Jake whispered.

Sure enough, it was the snake.

In the dim light, we watched the fat slithery bandit slide its slender ten-foot-long body out of the coop and pause, its ugly head swaying side to side. The face was paler than the rest of it. Greenish-brown eyes poked from its coffin-shaped head. Black specks were sprinkled along the back half of its greenish tail.

"Look," whispered Jake, "you can tell it's been swallowing eggs. Probably four or five of them. See? They're stuck in its throat."

Jake was right. The snake glided along to a small hole in the fence. It poked its head through, hoping to escape. But the eggs were bulging from its neck, holding it back. Mr. Mamba fought and thrashed until the eggs in its throat cracked one by one. Pop! Pop! Pop!

Then the burglar swallowed and vanished through the tall grass into the night.

I wanted Jake to say something. Finally, he did. "There's always something to be glad about."

"Like what?" I asked.

"Well, I'm glad snakes can't fly."

"Me too."

"In the rain forest of Borneo, they have a ribbon-flat paradise tree snake that glides from tree to tree like a flying squirrel."

"You're m-m-making that up."

"No, I'm not."

"D-d-do they live around here?" I asked, my eyes almost popping from my head, like eggs bulging in a snake's neck.

"Na," said Jake. "But there might be one in the zoo."

"You mean the zoo the black mamba escaped from?"

"Yep," he grinned. "That's the one."

"Jake?" I asked, staring through the branches. "Did you splatter eggs on the side of our house?"

"No." Jake moved a little so he could look through the branches. "What in the world?"

"I just saw it now," I said.

"Well, looks like Pete Wall and his gang have been up to no good," he said.

"What do you mean?"

"Eggs have been missing. I think there's more than one thief in Cluckingham Palace."

"What will we do?" I asked.

Jake was quiet.

"What will we do about the snake?"

Jake frowned and said, "I don't have a clue."

TO THINK ABOUT:

What was the scariest part of this chapter?

Jake says, "There's always something to be glad about." What are you glad about?

More than one thief is stealing eggs. What would you do?

Who should we go to when we're in trouble?

TO SMILE ABOUT:

Q: Why did the scrambled egg lose the baseball game?
A: The boiled eggs were hard to beat.

TO MEMORIZE:

"Call to me and I will answer you and tell you great and unsearchable things you do not know."

Jeremiah 33:3

LATE-NIGHT FEARS AND BEDTIME PRAYERS

During my bath I thought about our mamba problem. My tiny brain had solutions. None made sense. "Maybe you could shoot the snake," I told Jake, as I pulled on my PJs. Jake shook his head. "Our pellet gun isn't strong enough. It would just make the thing mad."

"What about poison, or a slingshot, or a trap?"

"They might work. But snakes are pretty smart. We've gotta outthink him."

I checked under my bed before crawling into it. And then the closet. And my dresser. And my shoes. I even checked the ceiling before turning off the light.

"If you corner a black mamba," said my brother from the bunk above mine, "it will raise its head off the ground about three feet and let out a hollow-sounding hiss. If that happens, just freeze. Don't move. They usually leave you alone. But if one attacks you, go tell Mom right away."

I wanted to turn the light back on, but it would mean walking back across the floor. What if our mamba was under the bed?

"Snakes smell with their tongues," said Jake. "They don't have eyelids and they can't blink. That's why they just seem to stare at you when you get close."

"J-J-Jake," I asked, "can we talk about something else?"

"Okay, Kiddo. I'm sorry."

"J-J-Jake? Why aren't you scared?"

At first I thought he was asleep, but finally he answered. "Sometimes I get frightened too. But I guess I've learned that… well, just a minute." I heard him fishing around for his flashlight, then flipping pages in the old book he read every day. "When we're afraid," Jake said, "we should remember that God won't leave us. Oh, here it is. 'God is our refuge and strength, an ever-present help in trouble'" (Psalm 46:1).

I could hear him flipping more pages. "The Bible tells us two more things we should do. Listen to this. 'Do not be anxious about anything, but in every situation, by prayer and petition, with thanksgiving, present your requests to God' (Philippians 4:6). I'll pray, then you give thanks.

"Dear God," Jake prayed, "help us outsmart the snake. Amen. Now it's your turn."

"Okay. Um…dear God, thanks that Jake said he's gonna clean those eggs off the house before I wake up. Amen."

Jake laughed. "I did," he said softly. "And I will. I set my alarm cluck. Goodnight."

"Goodnight."

Soon Jake was snoring softly like a tiny lawnmower, but not me. I lay awake in the dark, scared, thinking of Pete Wall's gang of mean-looking thugs and about poor Mrs. Wilson who hadn't had a bath in two weeks from worrying about finding that rotten snake. I didn't ever want to swim again in Crooked Creek. Or see a bathtub. Or pick eggs in Cluckingham Palace. My summer was being ruined by three bullies and a dumb old snake.

Suddenly, I thought of Jake's joke. And I got it! "Alarm clucks," I said out loud. I snickered. Jake woke up and said, "Dr. Pepper is not a real doctor." Then he was snoring again. I guess he didn't wake up at all. Like Dad said once, "Sometimes he sleeps in his talk."

As I drifted off, I prayed that God would make my big brother smarter so he'd think of something.

And the next day he did.

TO THINK ABOUT:

Do you know anyone who talks in their sleep?

When Jake is in trouble, he goes to the Bible for help. Why is that a good idea?

Can you remember the three things Jake said we should do when we're scared?

What would you like to pray about?

TO SMILE ABOUT:

Q: What is a snake's favourite school subject?
A: Hisstory.

TO MEMORIZE:

"In peace I will lie down and sleep, for you alone, Lord, make me dwell in safety."

Psalm 4:8

JAKE'S EGGSCELLENT PLAN

The alarm clock worked. Jake was up early, scraping eggs off the house then boiling two fresh ones for his breakfast. "I'll have mine fried," I said, and when they landed on my plate, I hid them under some golden-brown toast. But Mom wasn't blind.

"Eat two giant bites, Sweetie," she said, "and I'll bring you peanut butter and honey. If not, you can have the eggs for supper."

"Thith ith dithguthting," I said, swallowing the first bite. "Thith tathes like ticken featherth," I said, choking down the second.

Jake laughed. "Here's how to eat a hard-boiled egg," he said. "First tap it lightly on top, then peel off the part that cracks. Then do the same to the bottom. Like this. Then put it on its side on the table and roll it a bit. See? Then, cup the egg with one hand, put the top end in your mouth, and blow." The egg flew out of the shell and bounced across the table onto my plate.

I laughed so hard I almost choked.

Suddenly Jake had a faraway look. Then the widest grin spread across his face. "What's going on?" I asked.

"You'll never guess in a month of Tuesdays," said Jake. "Just you wait."

The grin was still there when we climbed back up the old oak tree to wait.

The sun changed into its jammies and slid slowly into bed. An owl hooted softly. A cricket kept its neighbours awake.

"Owls always hunt at night," said Jake. "I hear they can carry little kids away in their claws."

"I'm not a little kid," I said.

Half an hour passed. My rear end was so sore I felt like I was a hundred and fifty years old, like Grandpa. My eyelids wanted to shut too. "Maybe we should climb down," I said, yawning. "I don't want to fall asleep up here."

"I'll tell you some snake jokes," said Jake.

"No, please don't."

"What kind of snakes are found on cars?" I didn't know, so I kept quiet. "Windshield vipers," he said.

I had to think about that.

"Why couldn't the snake talk? Because he had a frog in his throat."

"That means he had a cold, right?"

Jake punched me softly on the shoulder. And we just sat there, smiling.

"Jake," I said, "I was thinking about what you said last night. About God being with us. I sometimes don't think so."

I felt another soft punch. "I know so," said Jake. "That's his promise. And he doesn't break them."

"You're my favourite little brother," he smiled. And we sat there some more. I was his *only* brother, but it was the happiest I've ever been. Up in a tree.

TO THINK ABOUT:

What's your favourite breakfast and why?

Would you like to try Jake's trick with a boiled egg? Who could help you?

Which was your favourite joke in this chapter?

Do you think God is with you? Why?

TO SMILE ABOUT:

**Q: What bird is with you for every meal?
A: A swallow.**

TO MEMORIZE:

"Trust in the Lord with all your heart and lean not on your own understanding; in all your ways submit to him, and he will make your paths straight."

Proverbs 3:5-6

THE THIEF'S SNEAKY SURPRISE

"Shhh," Jake whispered, holding a finger to his lips. "The snake's getting hungry, I just know it."

But for the first time ever, Jake was wrong.

Snap! A twig gave way beneath us. A voice said, "Nobody move!" I thought we'd been caught, but ever so slowly, three boys in dark clothes sneaked out from under the oak and crept toward Cluckingham Palace. "What should we do?" I whispered.

"Nothing. Just watch. Looks like the snake isn't the only egg thief."

Pete Wall led the way, twirling his head like an owl, half expecting to be caught. They reached the fence that was guarding the coop. Pete reached for the latch on the narrow doorway. The other two grabbed the gate and pulled.

If I live to be a hundred, I will never see anything like it.

All at once, they screamed. As if they had *eggsploded*. Running for the woods, they howled like a pack of wild hyenas. They ran fast. Faster than they ever thought they could. Crashing into trees. Tripping over logs. And yelling: "Ow! Ow! Ow!"

Finally, all was quiet. Except for Jake. He couldn't stop laughing.

"What happened? Tell me! Tell me!"

"Well," Jake said, "I asked Dad about electric fences, and he helped me hook up a battery to the wire. Not a big one. Not strong enough to hurt anyone. But when your conscience is guilty, everything seems scarier. Maybe they thought they got shot. What if they got into the coop and found the snake there?" The thought made him laugh even more.

Suddenly he raised his finger again. "Shhhh." The chickens grew restless. The clucking grew louder. "Help! Thief!" they seemed to say.

We watched the snake slip out of Cluckingham Palace, its ugly coffin head swaying from side to side. It didn't blink at all. I was pretty sure it could see us up in the tree.

"Look," I whispered. "More eggs...stuck in its throat."

The mamba slinked along to the small hole in the fence and poked its head through. It was a tight fit. "It'll be gone again," I said to Jake. "You better do something." But Jake wasn't there. Then I saw him. He had climbed quietly down and, from behind a tree, a great big guy joined him. Slowly they approached the coop. I hung on to a branch, almost too scared to watch.

The snake pushed and struggled, but there was no pop, pop, pop this time. It thrashed about wildly, trying to force its bulging neck through the tiny hole. Suddenly the big guy lowered a long pole and clamped a steel collar around the snake's head. "Gotcha Mac!" he yelled. "You'll be back in my zoo by bedtime."

Jake turned and looked up at me, that same old grin on his face. He looked triumphant, like a boy who had just outsmarted Mac the Mamba.

"How did you do it?" I asked, after the zookeeper backed Mac up, slid him into a cage, and drove away.

Jake didn't say anything at first. Just laughed until he had to sit down. "Hard-boiled eggs," he said at last. "My favourite."

I realized then that my hands hurt from holding onto the branches so tightly.

"Climb down," said my brother. "We have one more thing to do."

"What's that?"

"Someone hasn't had a bath in two weeks. The sun's still up. We can tell her it's safe now."

So I climbed down. And we laughed together all the way to Mrs. Wilson's house.

TO THINK ABOUT:

What's the first thing you will do now when you are afraid?

Jake talked to his dad about his problem. Why is that a good idea?

May this story help you learn to pray and trust God when life gets scary.

Let's pray about the things that frighten you. God will hear and answer.

TO SMILE ABOUT:

Jake: "Dad! He spilled milk on me!"
Dad: "How dairy!"

TO MEMORIZE:

"I sought the Lord, and he answered me; he delivered me from all my fears."

Psalm 34:4

MY PRAYER

I know that you made eggs, Lord,
But may I ask you why?
Jake cracks and smacks and wallops them,
And even makes them fry.

But still I often wonder
When looking to the sky,
Why can't they taste like ice cream
Poached on bumble berry pie?

MY VERY FIRST SONG

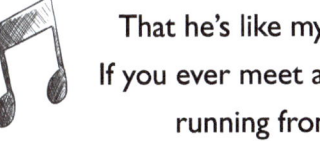

If you ever get a brother, make sure,
for goodness' sake,
That he's like my brother Jake.
If you ever meet a bully, or you're
running from a snake
Give your head a shake and call my brother Jake.

He cooks disgusting things, so you'll get a bellyache.
But he's rather nice to have around,
'cuz he can catch a snake.
So ask your father or your mother
for a great big brother.

Make very very awful sure he's like my brother Jake.
Give your head a shake, and call my brother Jake.
Just yell and he'll be there. He's my brother Jake.

JAKE'S GOODNIGHT PRAYER

Thank you, God, this day's gone by.

Thank you tons that snakes don't fly.

Thanks for brains and arms and legs.

And thank you, Lord, for hard-boiled eggs.

JAKE'S WAKE-UP PRAYER

I just awoke, here comes the light,
I know you kept me through the night.
Guard my little tongue today.
Forgive me, Lord, if I should stray.

Please help Pete and all the guys
To choose what's right and do what's wise.
And help my little brother to
Face his fears and trust in you.
Amen.

A FAMILY-FOCUSED INITIATIVE FROM LAUGH AGAIN!

Parents and grandparents are the two most influential people in the spiritual life of a child. That's why **Laugh Again Kids** exists: to support you in nurturing the spiritual growth of the young ones under your care. Laugh Again Kids offers resources and encouragement to help you engage and guide young people's faith journey with joy and wisdom.

Other books by **Laugh Again Kids**:

- *Jake and the Christmas Surprise*
- *Creation's Awesome Critters*
- *12 Days of Christmas Stories*

 CANADA: USA:

laughagain.ca/store   **laughagain.us/store**

Printed in the USA
CPSIA information can be obtained
at www.ICGtesting.com
JSHW041923250824
68706JS00001B/3